For my dad, who sang to me in the mornings, and his giant heart.

To Felicia for helping me embrace all the colors.

About This Book

The illustrations for this book were done in Holbein acrylic gouache and Prismacolor pencils on Arches 140 lb. hot press watercolor paper. This book was edited by Samantha Gentry and designed by Angelie Yap under the art direction of Saho Fujii. The production was supervised by Patricia Alvarado, and the production editors were Jen Graham and Jake Regier. The text was set in Plantin Std, and the display type is P22 Franklin Caslon.

In the Blue

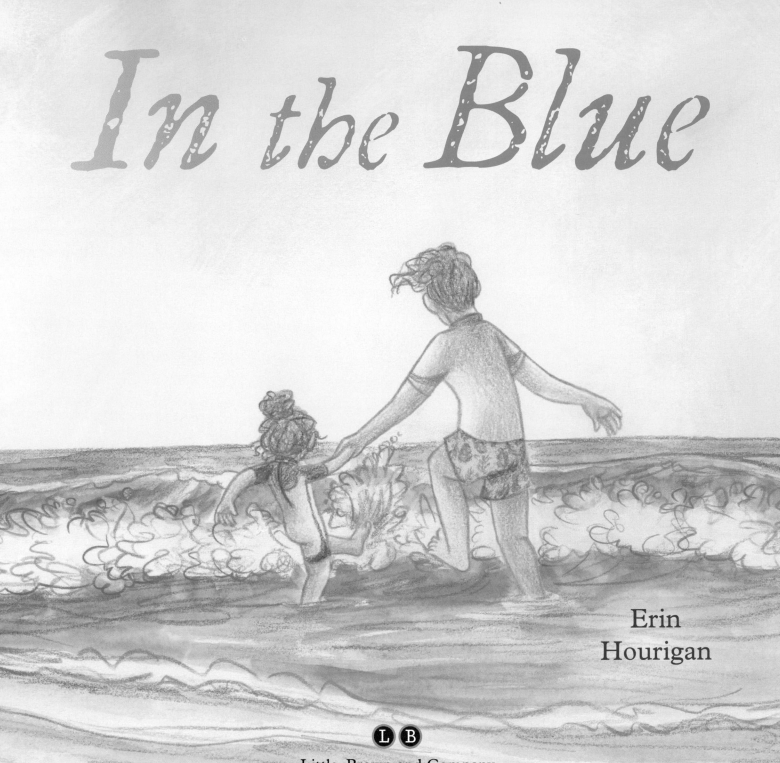

Erin
Hourigan

L B

Little, Brown and Company

New York Boston

My dad is as tall as the sky!

And I'm his teeny-tiny sunspot.

Even when storm clouds rumble,
he tells me that together,
we can do anything.

And we do.

In the morning, my dad fills my room with songs as bright as the sunrise.

At night, he tucks me in with kisses that reach up to the stars.

But right now, things for my dad aren't bright and yellow.
They are a deep, dark blue.

His kisses don't reach
as far at night,

and the morning is quiet and dim.

I try making him snacks and drawing him pictures.

For a second, the sun peeks through the clouds.

The next day, I try singing him songs and telling him stories.

But his face is a dark storm.

"Leave me be!" he roars. And the blue comes back.

I scream.

And rip.

Throw,

hit, and kick.

But it's no use.

My dad stays a
frozen, icy blue.

I'm afraid the other
colors are gone,

and I don't know what a
teeny-tiny sunspot can do.

So I whisper, "I love you," and
we all wait together in the blue.

When he's ready, my dad
visits people who help him.

I go, too.

We talk with someone who knows
all the colors, from sunny to midnight.

Soon the blue
grows lighter.

Until one night…

My dad's kisses climb
all the way back up to the stars.

After a while, he is bright and yellow again.

But the blue still comes back.
Sometimes in little drops, and
sometimes in big, crashing waves.
I know it won't ever completely go away.

But I'm not afraid.

Because whatever colors come our way, he'll always be my dad, as tall as the sky.

I'll always be his teeny-tiny sunspot.

And together, we can do anything.

Author's Note

When I was growing up, big emotions were all around me but not often talked about. Even after learning of my dad's clinical depression, I wasn't sure what to ask or say. Then I suffered a loss in my life, which started me on my own journey with depression. Writing this book was a way for me to talk about that experience and express those new feelings.

Although there is a lot of my own story here, we all have big emotions to work through from time to time. My hope is that this book will help open up conversations that can be difficult to start. When you're in the midst of depression or coping with loss, it can seem like you're the only one feeling the way you do. After reading this story, I hope you know you're not alone. And as scary and overwhelming as these big emotions can be, the more we talk about them and support one another, the better we will get at knowing and expressing all our colors and emotions, "from sunny to midnight."

Resources for Children and Families Coping with Mental Illness

Books

- *Balloons for Papa: A Story of Hope and Empathy* by Elizabeth Gilbert Bedia, illustrated by Erika Meza (HarperCollins, 2021)

- *Can I Catch It Like a Cold? Coping with a Parent's Depression* by Joe Weissmann (Tundra Books, 2009)

- *The Color Monster: A Story About Emotions* by Anna Llenas (Little, Brown Books for Young Readers, 2018)

- *The Color Thief: A Family's Story of Depression* by Andrew Fusek Peters and Polly Peters, illustrated by Karin Littlewood (Albert Whitman & Co., 2015)

- *Michael Rosen's Sad Book* by Michael Rosen, illustrated by Quentin Blake (Candlewick Press, 2005)

- *Sad Days, Glad Days: A Story About Depression* by DeWitt Hamilton, illustrated by Gail Owens (Albert Whitman & Co., 1995)

- *When Sadness Is at Your Door* by Eva Eland (Random House Books for Young Readers, 2019)

Websites

- **Families for Depression Awareness**
  https://familyaware.org
     A nonprofit organization dedicated to offering education, training, and a community to those who may be coping with bipolar disorders and depression.

- **National Alliance on Mental Illness (NAMI)**
  https://nami.org
     A grassroots organization dedicated to improving the lives of individuals and families affected by mental illness.

- **National Federation of Families**
  https://ffcmh.org
     A family-run organization dedicated to helping children with mental-health challenges and their families obtain support and services.

- **National Institute of Mental Health (NIMH)**
  https://nimh.nih.gov
     A federal organization dedicated to offering information on mental-health disorders and treatments.